This book is written
from the inspiration of
Bishop Marvin Sapp

Text and Illustration Copyrights © 2021 by Coral Lois Jones
All rights reserved, except as permitted under the U.S. Copyright Act of 1976.
No part of this publication may be reproduced, distributed, or transmitted in any form or by any means, or stored in a database or retrieval system, without the prior written permission of the publisher.

Contents

Statue of Liberty, Liberty Island Manhattan, New York City, New York. River House, Grand Rapids, Michigan. Fifth Third Center, Toledo, Ohio. Transamerica Tower, Baltimore, Maryland. PNC Plaza, Raleigh, North Carolina. Burnett Plaza, Fort Worth, Texas. Bank of America Plaza, Atlanta, Georgia. Eiffel Tower, Paris, France. Willis Tower, Chicago, Illinois. Empire State Building, Manhattan New York City, New York. One World Trade Center, New York, New York. Burj Khalifa, Dubai, Khalifa located in Burj Park by Emaar.

Lyniell was quickly walking his brother Cordaee to the FranThel Public Library when he bumped into Luis. Mouth agape. Luis asked, "Cordaee, is your brother a skyscraper?"

Cordaee said, "No, Luis, remember our teacher told us that a skyscraper is a tall building with stories, floors, and most skyscrapers are in cities. Not human beings!"

Luis asked, "Is your brother taller than the Statue of Liberty, that statue that stands on Liberty Island?"

Cordaee said, "Bro, in my brothers' history book, I saw a picture of the Statue of Liberty! This skyscraper symbolizes freedom for the immigrants coming across the sea! The broken shackle and chain on her foot signifies the end of slavery! No! My brother is not a skyscraper, but he is tall like one."

Statue of Liberty
Statue of Liberty
Statue of Liberty
Statue of Liberty
Statue of Liberty
Statue of Liberty

Luis asked, "Is your brother taller than River House? The tallest building in Grand Rapids, Michigan. That building is high! Its top floor is 397 ft. (121 meters), and its roof is 406 feet (124 meters) with 34 floors!"

Cordaee replied, "No, he is just tall like a skyscraper, but he is my brother!"

Luis further inquired, "Is your brother taller than the Fifth Third Center at One Seagate in Toledo, Ohio? That skyscraper is 411 ft. (125 m), tall and consist of 29 floors!"

Cordaee replied, "No, but did you know my mom talked about the Toledo Mud Hens, a minor league baseball team who plays inside Fifth Third Field! No, he is tall as a skyscraper; he is my brother!"

Luis asked, "Is your brother taller than The Transamerica Tower in Baltimore, Maryland? That skyscraper is 529 ft. (161 meters) and has 40 stories!"

Cordaee said, "No, he is just tall like a skyscraper, but he is my brother!"

Luis was curious and asked, "Is your brother taller than The PNC Plaza in Raleigh, North Carolina? That skyscraper is 538 ft. (164 m) with 33 stories, and it is the Nation's #1 producer of sweet potatoes!"

Cordaee said, "Uh! No, he is just tall like a skyscraper, but he is my brother!"

The PNC Plaza The PNC Plaza The PNC Plaza

Luis thought for a moment, then asked, "Is your brother taller than the Burnett Plaza in Fort Worth, Texas? That skyscraper is 567 ft. (173 m) tall and has 40 stories!"

Cordaee shook his head and said, "No, my brother is just tall like a skyscraper! Hey, did you know that Fort Worth is also called Cow Town?"

Luis further inquired, "Is your brother taller than the Bank of America Plaza skyscraper in Atlanta, Georgia? That skyscraper is a whopping 1,023 ft. (311m), tall, and has 55 floors!"

Cordaee replied, "Speaking about Atlanta, Hmmm... No, he is just tall like a skyscraper, but he is my brother!"

Luis continued with his questioning, "Is your brother taller than the Eiffel Tower in Paris, France? That skyscraper is 1,063 ft. (324 m) even though it has only three floors!"

Cordaee said, "No, he is just tall like a skyscraper, but he is my brother!"

Luis tapped his foot and scratched his chin as he tried to think of more buildings. Eventually, he said, "Is your brother taller than the Willis Tower in Chicago, Illinois. That skyscraper is 1,451 ft. (442 m), 110 floors!"

Cordaee replied, "Chicago is the state with the hot air politician, thus the Windy City is how it got its name! Oh, no he is just tall like a skyscraper!"

Willis Tower Willis Tower
Willis Tower Willis Tower
Willis Tower Willis Tower

Luis raised another inquiry saying, "Is your brother taller than the Empire State Building in Manhattan, New York City? That skyscraper is 1,454 ft. (443.2 m), tall, and has 102 floors!"

Cordaee said, "No, he is tall as a skyscraper, but he is my brother!"

Empire

State

Building

Luis then asked, "Is your brother taller than the One World Trade Center in New York, New York? That skyscraper is an incredible 1,776 ft. (541 m) with 104 stories! Did you know this is the tallest building in the United States?"

Cordaee said, "No, he is tall as a skyscraper, but he is my brother!"

One World Trade Center

Luis then asked, "Is your brother taller than the Burj Khalifa? That Skyscraper is 2,717 ft. (828 m) tall and has an amazing 163 floors! It's the tallest skyscraper in the world!"

Cordaee said, "No, he is tall as a skyscraper, but he is my brother!"

Burj Khalifa

Burj Khalifa

Eventually, Lyniell came to pick up Cordaee from the FranThel Public Library. He said, "You ready? How was your day?"

Luis jumped up and down.

"Wow, your brother is a skyscraper! I want a tower brother, too! One that I can applaud!" Cordaee laughed. "My mother said if he keeps eating and growing tall, he is going to eat us out of our house!" Cordaee exclaimed, "One day, I am going to be tall just like him and have a great career! You wait and see! See you tomorrow, Luis!"

Skyscraper Skyscraper Skyscraper Skyscraper Skyscraper

Measurement Key

Customary

1 mile (mi) = 1,760 yards (yd)

1 yard (yd) = 3 feet (ft)

1 foot (ft) = 12 inches (in.)

Metric

1 kilometer (km) = 1,000 meters (m)

1 meter (m) = 100 centimeters (cm)

1 centimeter (cm) = 10 millimeters (mm)

CPSIA information can be obtained
at www.ICGtesting.com
Printed in the USA
LVHW072314141021
700524LV00002B/30